HOMEGOING:
A children's book about grief

chelsea c. mclin

Dedicated to my granny,
Rosie Mae Tanner.
1930 - 2020

Jubilee Books

ISBN 9780578910031 (hardcover)

Illustrations copyright © 2021 by Chelsea C. McLin
Cover Design by Chelsea McLin

Printed by IngramSpark in the United States of America

Jubilee Books
Silver Spring, MD

www.jubileebooks.shop

My granny is my favorite person in the whole universe.

She gives the best hugs,
makes the best treats, and...

She loves to play dress-up
with me and go on fun
adventures.

But we don't get to go on adventures anymore...

One day, all of our friends and family came to our house with food and flowers.

There was lots of crying and hugging.

Mama and Daddy
even made a speech and thanked
everyone for coming to Granny's
homegoing service.

Homegoing? Granny lived with Mama, Daddy, Baby Sister, and me. I didn't want her to go away.

If Granny moved away, I would visit her.

I wondered what Granny's new home looked like. Did she live on a big farm with lots of animals?

Home is where the barn is!

Or maybe she lived in a cottage with a garden full of fruits and vegetables?

Wherever Granny lived, I knew she'd be enjoying her favorite cup of coffee and reading the news.

I packed an extra can from the kitchen and a newspaper so she wouldn't miss any important stories.

I couldn't wait to visit Granny at her new home, but when I asked Mama to drive me, she said, "It's not a place you can visit by car."

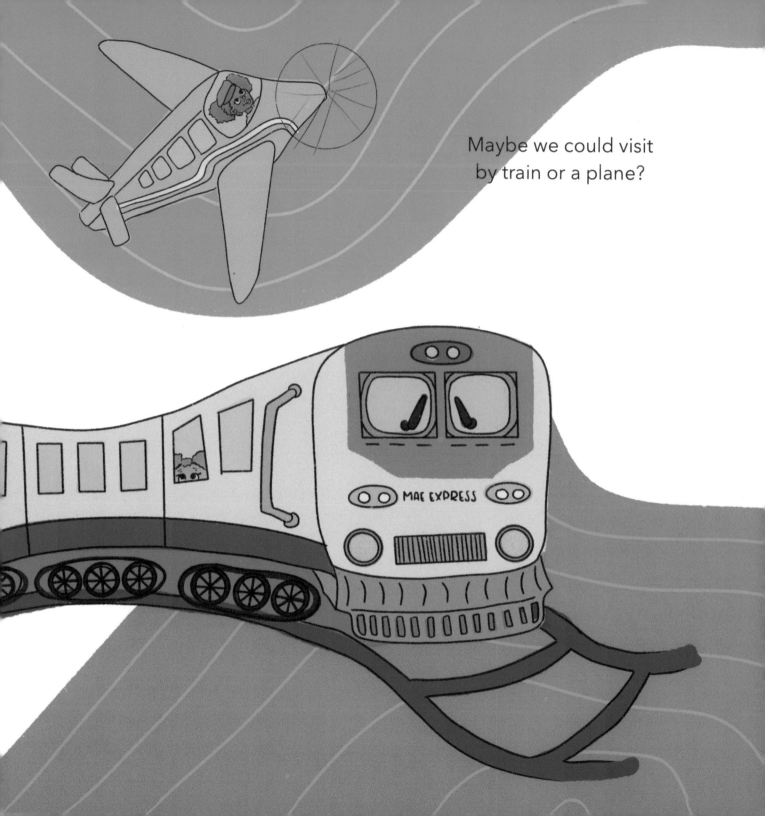

Maybe we could visit
by train or a plane?

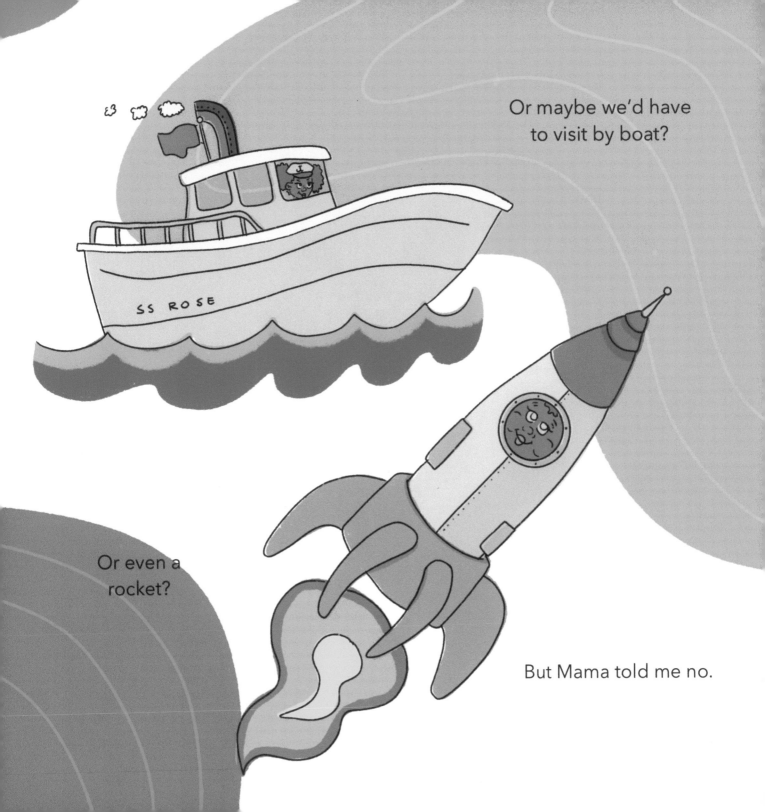

Or maybe we'd have to visit by boat?

Or even a rocket?

But Mama told me no.

It frustrated me that I couldn't visit Granny, but then I thought, "I could write her a letter!" I found some paper and an envelope, and I started to write.

When I asked Mama for a stamp to send the letter, she said, "It's not a place that accepts mail, either."

She told me that Granny lived a very long life, and she passed away. Granny's heart worked hard.

It helped her go on walks in the morning,

to dance at birthday parties,

and most importantly, to love all of us. But now the time had come for her heart to rest.

At first, I was angry.

I was confused.

But mostly, I was sad. I couldn't think about Granny without feeling hurt.

I asked Mama, "If Granny passed away, why did you say she 'went home?'"

Mama said, "We call it 'going home' because it gives us peace and comfort to believe her spirit has returned to a better place not on earth."

"I like to think that Granny is in the stars."

Mama said, "It's okay to think of Granny and your wonderful memories. It may feel bad at first, but over time that feeling will fade."

She was right. I miss my granny, but I'm not so sad anymore.

I remember how much she loved me and how much I loved her, and I feel okay. One day when I'm a granny, too, we'll be home together in the stars.

CPSIA information can be obtained
at www.ICGtesting.com
Printed in the USA
LVHW071309180222
711474LV00007B/94